Dear Parent,

Going to day care or preschool for the very first time or returning to school each September is both exciting and frightening to a child. *Word Bird's School Words* is a wonderful story to read in preparation for this big day.

In *Word Bird's School Words*, Word Bird creates a special word house just for words relating to school, such as books and teacher. You and your child can help Word Bird create more school words and deposit them in the Word House. If you haven't done so already, make your own Word House together. You might use the box in which these books arrived or a shoe box.

As a special treat, take your child to the school supplies section of a store. There, the two of you will be able to look at many school items and think of new words to put into your Word House. If possible, buy a set of crayons, a pencil or a lunch box to let your child know that going to school is something very special!

Word Bird's Friend,

Jane Belk Moncure

Learn to Read with **Word Bird** EARLY WORDS

WORD BIRD'S
SCHOOL WORDS

by
Jane Belk Moncure

illustrated by
Linda Sommers Hohag

NEWFIELD
PUBLICATIONS
SHELTON, CONNECTICUT

Published by arrangement with The Child's World, Inc.
Newfield Publications and design are federally registered
trademarks of Newfield Publications, Inc.

1995 Edition

Library of Congress Cataloging in Publication Data

Moncure, Jane Belk.
    Word Bird's school words/by Jane Belk Moncure; illustrated by
Linda Hohag.
    p. cm. - (Word house words for early birds)
    Summary: Word Bird puts words about school in his word house,
introducing such words as "teacher," "school bus," "books," and others.
    ISBN 0-89565-510-1
    1. Vocabulary—Juvenile literature. 2. Schools—Juvenile
literature. [1. Schools.   2. Vocabulary.]   I. Hohag, Linda, ill.
II. Title.   III. Series: Moncure, Jane Belk.   Word house words
for early birds.
PE1449.M5296   1989
428.1-dc20   89-7179   CIP   AC

Word Bird made a...

word house.

"I will put school words
in my house," he said.

He put in these words—

Back-to-School
SALE

school clothes

school supplies

school friends

school bus

safety patrol

teacher

backpack

lockers

building blocks

play store

paints

puzzles

library

books

story

puppets

pets

field trip

lunchtime

games

music

marching

playground

recess

Can you read these schoo

school clothes

lockers

school supplies

building blocks

school friends

play store

school bus

paints

safety patrol

puzzles

teacher

library

backpack

words with  ?

lunchtime

books

games

story

music

puppets

marching

pets

playground

field trip

recess

31

You can make a school word house. You can put Word Bird's words in your house and read them too.

Can you think of other school words to put in your word house?